MW00885610

TUMMY RUMBLE QUAKE

written by Heather L. Beal
illustrated by Jubayda Sagor

Thank you to my family, especially my husband, who always supports my efforts to rock the world.

Leileiana and Nickolai, I love you and thank you daily for teaching me about the world through your eyes.

For all the children out there, I want to tip the odds in YOUR favor. I hope this book helps you become stronger through reading. – Heather

TRAIN 4 SAFETY PRESS
BREMERTON, WA

Text and illustrations copyright © 2017 by Heather L. Beal. All rights reserved. Except as permitted under the United States Copyright Act of 1976, no part of this book may be reproduced, stored in or introduced into a retrieval system or transmitted, in any form, or by any means (electronic or mechanical, photocopying, recording, or otherwise), without the prior written permission of both the copyright owner and the publisher of this book.

ISBN 978-0-9987912-5-8 (hardback)
ISBN 978-0-9987912-2-7 (paperback)
ISBN 978-0-9987912-3-4 (e-book)

Library of Congress Control Number: 2017908993

Publisher's Cataloging-in-Publication data

Names: Beal, Heather L., author. I Sagor, Jubayda, illustrator.
Title: Tummy rumble quake / written by Heather L. Beal ; illustrated by Jubayda Sagor.
Description: Bremerton, WA: Train 4 Safety Press, 2017.
Identifiers: ISBN 978-0-9987912-2-7 (pbk.) I 978-0-9987912-3-4 (e-book) I LCCN 2017908993
Summary: Lily and Niko's childcare class learns about earthquakes and about the Great ShakeOut. They learn how to be safe during an earthquake.
Subjects: LCSH Earthquakes--Juvenile fiction. I Accidents--Prevention--Juvenile fiction. I Safety education--Juvenile fiction. I BISAC JUVENILE FICTION / Nature & the Natural World / Environment
Classification: LCC PZ7.B356835 Tum 2017I DDC [E]--dc23

Ms. Mandy went to the bookcase and shook it.

"What are you doing?" asked Lily.

Ms. Mandy shook the bookcase again. "The Great ShakeOut.™ is tomorrow, so I am making sure the bookcase is securely attached to the wall."

Niko scratched his head. "The Great ShakeOut?™"

Dylan jumped up. "I know! It's when everyone practices for earthquakes. My big brother's class did that last year."

"What's an earthquake?" asked Niko.

"An earthquake," Ms. Mandy explained, "is when the ground shakes so much that buildings and things inside them can fall or break."

"Why does it do that?" asked Lily.

"It happens because the earth is made up of big rocks, called plates," said Ms. Mandy. "They fit together like a puzzle, but they don't always play nice. Sometimes they want to be in the same spot at the same time, so they push and shove each other. Earthquakes can happen where these plates touch."

Ciena frowned. "Why doesn't someone tell them to take turns?"

Ms. Mandy let out a little laugh. "I wish someone could."

"How do you know if there's an earthquake?" asked Lily.

"If it's strong enough," said Ms. Mandy, "everything moves or shakes. You may even fall down. And, sometimes there's a loud, rumbly sound."

Niko held his stomach. "My tummy makes rumbly sounds when I'm hungry. Does it sound like that?"

"An earthquake is much louder than your tummy," said Ms. Mandy.

"Ms. Mandy," asked Ciena, "What should we do if there's an earthquake?"

"Three things," said Ms.Mandy. "Drop, cover, and hold on."

"First drop to the ground," directed Ms. Mandy.

"Should we lay down?" asked Lily.

Ms. Mandy shook her head. "No, Lily. You should get on your hands and knees. That way you can crawl away if needed."

"Next, we cover," said Ms. Mandy.

"If you're near a desk, table, or bed, crawl under it and cover your head with one hand. If you can't get under anything, go to an inside wall and cover your head with both hands."

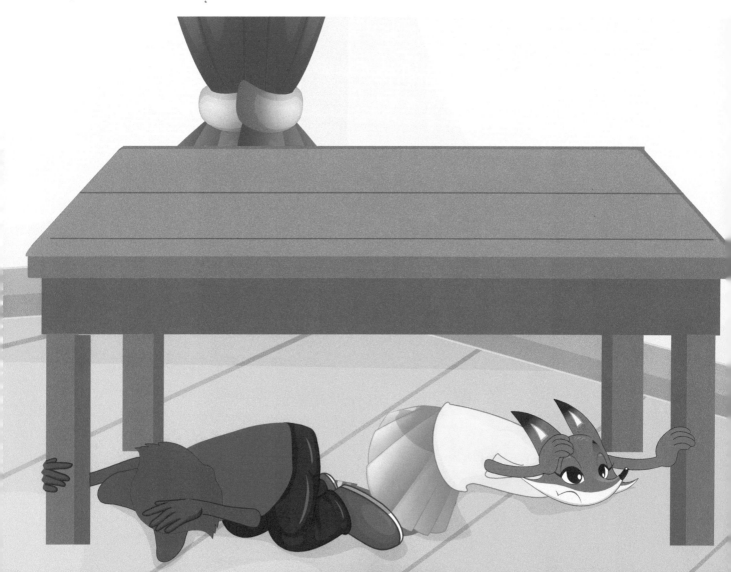

"Last thing is to hold on. If you're under furniture hold on to it with your free hand until the shaking stops."

Ms. Mandy walked to the back of the room. "Now look around. Is anything on the wall above you?"

Lily nodded.

"Then move away," said Ms. Mandy. "Earthquakes can knock things off the walls and knock over heavy things. If you're near bookcases, refrigerators, or tall furniture, move away."

Niko scratched his head again. "That's a lot to remember."

"Yeah," said Lily. "Do you have a song to help?"

Ms. Mandy smiled. "I do. Everyone repeat after me.

"If the room starts to rock, stop what you're doing and drop.
Get under cover on the floor; hold on till it's safe once more."

The kids sang the song and practiced drop, cover, and hold on.

Lily got up and brushed her clothes off. "Ms. Mandy, are we ready for the Great ShakeOut™ now?"

"Almost." said Ms. Mandy as she led the class to the playground. "We need to talk about a few more things."

"What do you think is the first thing to do if we feel an earthquake when we're outside?" asked Ms. Mandy.

"Drop, cover, and hold on," the class yelled together.

"Very good," said Ms. Mandy. "Move away from trees and buildings then drop and cover your head with both hands."

Roman raised his hand up high. "What if we're in a car?"

Ms. Mandy nodded. "Good question, Roman. The grownup driving will pull over and turn off the car. You should stay in the car until a grownup tells you it's safe."

"What do we do after the earthquake?" asked Ciena.

"After an earthquake, there may be more, smaller, earthquakes called after-shocks," said Ms. Mandy. "A grown up will tell you when it's safe to move and where to go. Are you ready to practice one more time for the Great ShakeOut?™"

Niko's tummy rumbled loudly. "Can we practice after lunch?"

"Yes, Niko," said Ms. Mandy as the kids laughed. "You all did a great job learning about being prepared for earthquakes."

"I like learning how to be prepared," said Niko. "But I especially like lunch time."

CPSIA information can be obtained
at www.ICGtesting.com
Printed in the USA
LVHW070044270819
628924LV00014B/526/P